Walt Disney's THE JUNGLE Book

Illustrated by the Disney Storybook Artists
Adapted by Kate Hannigan

© Disney Enterprises, Inc.
Visit our Web site at www.disneybooks.com

Published by
Louis Weber, C.E.O.
Publications International, Ltd.
7373 North Cicero Avenue
Lincolnwood, Illinois 60712

www.pilbooks.com

Manufactured in China.

8 7 6 5 4 3 2 1

ISBN: 0-7853-9545-8

On a dark night deep in the jungle, a black panther
named Bagheera was on the prowl. He was looking
for food when he heard a strange noise. Bagheera followed
the cry and found a baby in a basket. "A man-cub!
Someone must take care of it!" he said.

Bagheera knew of a family of wolves with many young
cubs. "What is one more mouth to feed?" he wondered.
And that is how Mowgli came to be raised as a cub in the
wolf pack.

The rainy seasons came and went ten times. Mowgli grew into a boy. Even though the wolves loved him, they wanted Mowgli to leave the jungle before the great tiger called Shere Khan found him. Shere Khan did not want Man in his jungle, and the wolves feared they could not protect Mowgli from him.

Bagheera told the wolves that he knew of a man-village where Mowgli would be safe. The wolves would miss Mowgli, but they knew it was for the best. So Mowgli and Bagheera set off in search of the man-village.

Bagheera and Mowgli walked deeper and deeper into the jungle. When Mowgli grew tired, they stopped for the night and slept in the thick branches of a tree. Just as they were drifting off to sleep, Kaa the snake appeared.

Kaa was hungry and thought the man-cub would make a tasty morsel. Staring into Mowgli's eyes, Kaa lulled him into a trance. Mowgli was hypnotized! Kaa slowly wrapped his coils around Mowgli and began to squeeze.

Bagheera woke up just in time! "Kaa! Kaa! Let him go!"
he shouted. And with a swipe of his mighty paw, the
panther knocked the snake on the head and freed Mowgli.
Kaa fell from the tree with a crash. He was furious!

"You've made a stupid mistake," Kaa hissed. He slithered
away as best he could, but his tail was tied up in a knot!

Bagheera was worried about Mowgli, but he wasn't
afraid of Kaa. "Now go to sleep, Mowgli," he said.

Mowgli loved the jungle and did not want to live in a man-village. He decided to run away. When morning came, he jumped from the tree and joined a parade of elephants passing below. The elephants marched in a row and then lined up for inspection.

Colonel Hathi, the leader of the elephants, examined his troops. He came across Mowgli standing at attention at the end of the line. "What happened to your trunk?" Colonel Hathi asked. When he realized that Mowgli was a man-cub, he was outraged!

Bagheera, once again, ran to Mowgli's rescue, helping
him down from the elephant's trunk. Bagheera told
Colonel Hathi that he was taking Mowgli back to the
man-village — to stay.

Colonel Hathi called his troops to attention and
marched them off into the jungle. Bagheera tried to do the
same with Mowgli, but the man-cub didn't want to go.

The panther grew frustrated. "That does it!" said
Bagheera. "I've had it!"

"Don't worry about me," Mowgli said. "I'll be just fine."

Mowgli was on his own in the jungle after Bagheera left him. Before long, he came across a happy-go-lucky bear called Baloo. Baloo loved to have a good time, so he and Mowgli spent the day splashing in the river, picking bananas, and climbing trees.

Baloo wanted to help Mowgli survive in the jungle. He showed him how to fight like a bear, and he taught him how to growl like one, too. "Like this, from your toes," Baloo said. Then he let out a roar that shook the trees.

Mowgli tried to roar like Baloo, but he wasn't loud enough. Finally, he got the hang of it. Mowgli took a deep breath and growled. His growl echoed through the jungle and reached the ears of Bagheera far away.

Bagheera thought Mowgli was in danger! He raced back through the trees and found the man-cub playing happily with his new friend. Bagheera rolled his eyes. "It's just Baloo, that lazy bear," he said to himself.

Baloo liked Mowgli and said he didn't have to return to the man-village. Baloo said Mowgli could live with him. Mowgli was excited, and he climbed onto Baloo's big back and gave him a hug. The two friends laughed and wrestled, tumbling right into the river. They floated in the water and drifted lazily downstream.

Before long, some monkeys began to watch Baloo and Mowgli from the treetops. Dangling from branches by their long tails, the monkeys waited for Baloo and Mowgli to float by. In a flash, they reached down and snatched Mowgli right off Baloo's big belly!

"Bagheera, help!" shouted Baloo. The monkeys had run off with Mowgli, and Baloo didn't know how to get him back. Bagheera knew just where to go. Before long, Bagheera and Baloo found the man-cub and helped him escape from the tricky monkeys.

That night they had a long talk. "Now do you see why Mowgli has to leave the jungle?" Bagheera asked Baloo.

Baloo loved Mowgli as if he were his own little cub. But he knew Bagheera was right. Mowgli would have to leave the jungle before Shere Khan found him. But Mowgli didn't want to go.

"Don't you realize you're human?" Baloo asked Mowgli.

"Not anymore, Baloo. Now I'm a bear like you!" answered Mowgli.

Baloo was getting frustrated. Finally he told Mowgli that he was going to take him to the man-village himself. Mowgli was angry and ran away. He had thought Baloo was going to let him stay in the jungle.

Bagheera and Baloo searched for Mowgli everywhere. They ran to the elephants and asked them to help find Mowgli before it was too late. Bagheera told Colonel Hathi that Shere Khan was sure to pick up the man-cub's trail. As the panther spoke, someone was lurking and listening in the deep brush. It was the dreaded Shere Khan, and he heard everything.

The great tiger laughed to himself. He knew he was getting closer and closer to finding the man-cub.

Mowgli wandered alone in the jungle. He was sad without Baloo and Bagheera. Soon the sly old snake Kaa slithered by. He tried to hypnotize Mowgli again. As Kaa stared into Mowgli's eyes, he slowly wrapped his coils around the man-cub.

Kaa was just about to sink his teeth into Mowgli when Shere Khan stopped by for a visit. He asked Kaa who he was talking to. Kaa tried to hide Mowgli, but the great tiger sensed the man-cub was near.

The snake didn't want to share Mowgli with anyone, so he quietly let him go. "That tiger gives me the shivers," he hissed to himself.

Mowgli walked on in the jungle to a lonely place. He was thinking about his old friends when he made a few new ones. Some kind vultures tried to cheer Mowgli up.

Just as Mowgli began to feel a little better, he ran right into the great tiger! Shere Khan had finally found him.

"I'm not afraid of you!" Mowgli shouted bravely to the tiger.

Shere Khan growled. He wanted the man-cub out of his jungle right away. He tried to chase Mowgli, but suddenly Baloo appeared! The big bear grabbed Shere Khan's tail and pulled with all his might. Baloo saved Mowgli!

The vultures swooped down and carried Mowgli to safety in an old tree. Shere Khan was angry that the man-cub had escaped. He snarled at Baloo and began to run after him. "I have to help Baloo!" cried Mowgli.

Just then a storm kicked up, and thunder crashed in the sky. Lightning struck a nearby tree and started a small fire. Mowgli grabbed a burning branch and tied it to Shere Khan's tail. The great tiger was terrified! He ran from the jungle and never returned.

Mowgli was a hero! The vultures cheered, but Mowgli was sad. He was afraid Bagheera and Baloo were still going to take him to the man-village.

"Nobody's ever going to come between us again!" said Baloo. He swung his little friend in his arms and gave him a big bear hug. With Shere Khan gone from the jungle, Baloo knew Mowgli could stay.

Just then, Mowgli heard a beautiful sound drifting through the trees. It was unlike anything he'd ever heard before, and it was coming from a clearing nearby. Mowgli climbed up a tall tree for a better look.

"What is that lovely sound?" he asked.

It was a girl from the man-village. She was singing as she tied a bow in her shiny hair. Mowgli was fascinated. As she walked away, Mowgli began to follow her. She was returning to the man-village!

Mowgli stopped on the trail and looked back at his friends Baloo and Bagheera. The panther told Mowgli to go on. Mowgli waved to them, then he turned and followed the girl to the gates of the man-village.

Bagheera and Baloo waved good-bye to Mowgli. They were sad to see their friend leave them. But it was for the best. He would be at home in the man-village, they said.

"Mowgli is where he belongs now," Bagheera told Baloo. The big bear sniffed and wiped his eyes. He agreed with Bagheera, but he still thought the little man-cub would have made a pretty good bear after all.